This book belongs to:

Mr Wolf's Guide to Royal Etiquette

Firstly you will need:

a crown   or a tiara

and a throne

There's a right way to wear a crown . . . and a wrong way

Good posture is *frightfully important*

A pair of glass slippers is handy for dancing

It's essential to wear
BIG sunglasses . . .

. . . and adorn yourself
with baubles and trinkets

bling! bling!

You will also need:

a castle

a fancy aeroplane

a swimming pool

a swanky boat

a fast car

But avoid all of these things:

axes

guillotines

dark towers
(especially in
London, England)

and anyone who looks like this . . .

For Peggy-Jane, Martin and Rosie
With love

And a huge, hairy, heartfelt thank you to
Tiffany, Cally and Kate – and Punter!

Mr Wolf can be contacted at
www.hungry-wolf.com

First published in Great Britain 2004 by Egmont Books Limited
239 Kensington High Street, London W8 6SA

Copyright © Jan Fearnley 2004

Jan Fearnley has asserted the moral right to be identified
as the author and illustrator of this book

A CIP catalogue record for this title is available from The British Library

Printed and bound in Italy

3 5 7 9 10 8 6 4

Hardback ISBN 1 4052 0539 3

Paperback ISBN 1 4052 1580 1

Mr Wolf and the Enormous Turnip

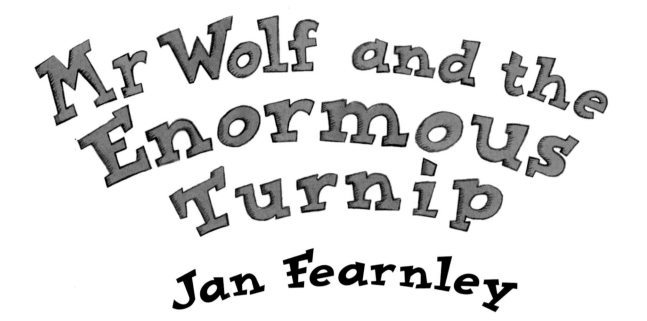

Jan Fearnley

EGMONT

One day, Mr Wolf found a most
peculiar thing in his garden.
It was a great big enormous turnip.

"Yum, yum!" he said,
licking his lips at the thought
of spicy turnip stew for supper.

He rubbed his paws together and set about picking the turnip.

But even though he *pulled* and *tugged*,
the turnip would not move.
Suddenly, a croaky little voice called out from
behind the bushes.
"Won't somebody help me, please?"

It was a little frog.
And he had a very sad tale to tell.

"Once I was a handsome prince. Then a horrible witch cast a spell on me and now I'm a frog," said the frog.
"Only a kiss from a princess will break the spell. Please help."

Mr Wolf's tummy rumbled long and loud. He looked at the turnip.

"If you help me," said the frog, noticing Mr Wolf's hesitation, "I'll command my servants to pull up your turnip."

"What a nice little frog," thought Mr Wolf. "I'll do what I can."

Mr Wolf took the frog to the royal palace where the beautiful princesses lived.

"I'm sure we can persuade a princess to kiss you better," he said.

They found the first princess in a royal chamber.
Minstrels serenaded her with sweet music as she pranced
about, admiring herself.

Mr Wolf bowed his best royal bow and said,
"Your Royal Highness, a witch cast a spell on this prince.
Please will you kiss him better?"

"Get lost!" said the princess.
"I'm not kissing a slimy frog!"

"Perhaps I can tempt you with some turnip stew,"
said Mr Wolf, his tummy rumbling at the very thought of it . . .

"I don't want stew from the likes of you," scoffed the princess.

"Never mind her," said the cat with the fiddle.
"She's awfully vain. But what about me?
I'm a *royal* cat. You can trace
my ancestry right back
to the Egyptians. For a
bowl of turnip stew,
I'll kiss him better."

Everyone agreed it was worth a try.
So, the cat kissed the frog.

NOTHING HAPPENED.

"Oh no!" cried the frog. "I am doomed to be froggy for ever."

"Don't give up," said the cat.
"She's not our only princess. Follow me."

The second princess was relaxing
in the palace gardens.
Mr Wolf bowed his best royal bow.
"Your Royal Highness," he said.
"A cruel witch cast a spell
on this handsome prince.
Please, *please* will you kiss
him better?"

"He'll give you some of his
turnip stew," added the frog.

"**Can't you see I'm busy?**" shouted the princess.
"Anyway, I *hate* turnip stew."

"Don't mind her," said the servant goose.
"She's very lazy. But how about me?
I'm a *royal* goose.
I can lay golden eggs.
For a bowl of turnip stew,
I'll kiss him."

So, the goose kissed the frog.

AND ABSOLUTELY NOTHING HAPPENED.

The frog was very upset.
"Cheer up," said the goose. "Follow me to the royal garage."

But the garage was cold and grimy, and quite empty except for a girl in overalls tinkering with a car.
"This is no place to find a princess!" grumbled the frog. Mr Wolf's tummy rumbled. He looked closely at the girl.

She wasn't very fancy, but she was a princess!

Mr Wolf bowed his best royal bow (he was getting rather good at it now) and said, "Your Royal Highness! A nasty, wicked witch cast a spell on this delightful, charming prince. Please, please, *please*, kiss him better."

The princess blew her nose on an oily rag.
"What's in it for me?" she said.
"A delicious bowl of turnip stew!" replied Mr Wolf.
"I love turnip stew!" said the princess.
"Yum, yum!"

"You don't look like
a princess to me," said the frog.

"Hush up, frog,
and hold still!"
commanded the princess.

. . . SHAZAM!

There stood a handsome prince.
He was absolutely splendid.

Mr Wolf was very impressed.

"Your Royal Highness,
Mr Prince, Sir,"
he said politely,
"now it's your turn
to help me."

"Oh, no," said the prince.
"It's simply not done for a noble prince to be seen
consorting with common wolves
and grubby old turnips.
Out of my way,
before I throw you
in my dungeons!"

"What a waste of a kiss," said the princess, in disgust.
"And still no turnip stew," said Mr Wolf.

It was time for drastic action.
Mr Wolf telephoned the witch
who had made the spell.

"We're having problems with our prince," he said. "He's *mean* and *nasty* and he doesn't keep his promises."

"I know," replied the witch. "That's why I magicked him in the first place."

"Can't you change him back?" asked Mr Wolf.

FREE TROLL WITH EVERY BROOM SOLD!

NO REFUNDS
NO RETURNS

ALL SPELLS SOLD AS SEEN

So be careful what you wish for!

BOGEYMAN SALE! (slightly soiled)

HUBBLE BUBBLE COUGH DROPS

HOCUS POCUS Computers

"Sorry," said the witch. "I'm afraid you are stuck with him."

"Oh, no," sighed Mr Wolf.
"Oh, no!" shrieked the princess.
"Those rascals are stealing my car!"

Mr Wolf thought very hard for a moment.
There was only one decent thing to do.

HE GOBBLED THE ROTTEN PRINCE UP!
And the horrid princesses, too!

SNAPPETY!

SNAP!

SNAP!

"Good riddance to the lot of them," said the nice princess, and she gave Mr Wolf a big hug and a . . .

kissy kiss kiss

"Now let's go and pick that turnip!" said Mr Wolf.

Together, Mr Wolf and his new friends *pulled* and *tugged*,
heaved and *huffed*. And finally . . .

POP!

. . . out came the turnip!

There was plenty of spicy stew for everyone.
And even though he'd already had a right royal feast,
Mr Wolf had an extra big helping.

Yum, yum!

Mr Wolf's Guide
to Royal Etiquette
Continued

It's important to appreciate the finer things in life:

counting your MONEY

prancing about in REGAL FINERY

EATING BON-BONS from a silver tray

waving to the COMMON CROWD

Shop 'til you pop

And SHOPPING of course!

Take time to enjoy the Arts:

I · LVPVS

OPERA

BALLET

and FINE MUSIC

Make sure that you and your friends
practise being TOFFEE-NOSED every day

A nap is always a relaxing diversion

Topiary is a pleasant pursuit
as is Gardening.

NB: Whilst busy in the garden,
do not become distracted by Royalty
masquerading as frogs
with a sob-story . . .

. . . It's best not to get involved

Other picture book titles by Jan Fearnley:

Mr Wolf and the Three Bears
1 4052 1582 8

Mr Wolf's Pancakes
1 4052 1581 X

A Special Something
0 7497 4639 4

Little Robin Red Vest
0 7497 3184 2
Board Book: 1 4052 1585 2

Just Like You
0 7497 4231 3

A Perfect Day For It
1 4052 0176 2

Blue Banana titles:

Mabel and Max
0 7497 3215 6

Colin and the Curly Claw
0 7497 4646 7